# The SIGN ON ROSIE'S DOOR

The SIGN on

# ROSIE'S DOOR

*Story and pictures by* MAURICE SENDAK

HARPER COLLINS PUBLISHERS    NEW YORK

Remembering *Pearl Karchawer*
*all the Rosies*
*and Brooklyn*

CHAPTER ONE

There was a sign on Rosie's door.

It read, "If you want to know a secret, knock three times."

Kathy knocked three times and Rosie opened the door.

"Hello, Kathy."

"Hello, Rosie. What's the secret?"

"I'm not Rosie any more," said Rosie. "That's the secret."

"Then who are you?" asked Kathy.

"I'm Alinda, the lovely lady singer."

"Oh," said Kathy.

6

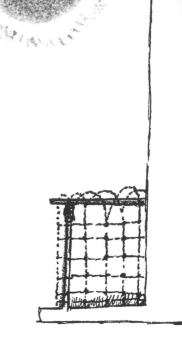

"And someday," said Rosie, "I'll sing in
a great musical show."

"When?" Kathy asked.

"Now, in my back yard. Want to come?"

"Can I be somebody too?" asked Kathy.

Rosie had to think for a minute.

"I suppose," she said finally, "you can be
Cha-Charoo, my Arabian dancing girl."

"All right," said Kathy. "I'll come."

And everybody came. Dolly and Pudgy
and Sal.

"Now sit down everybody," Rosie said.

They all sat down on folding chairs.

"Now keep quiet everybody," said Rosie.
"The show is going to begin."

They all sat quietly. Rosie and Kathy
disappeared behind the cellar door.

"This is a good show," Pudgy whispered.

"It is," said Dolly.

BAM, BAM, BAM! came the sound of a drum from behind the cellar door.

"Ladies and gentlemen!" cried a faraway voice. "We have for your pleasure Cha-Charoo, the Arabian dancing girl. Clap and shout hooray!"

Everybody shouted and clapped. The cellar door opened and Kathy stepped out. She wore a nightgown and had a towel over her head. She waved her arms and took three little steps.

"Cha-Charoo-roo-roo," she sang softly.

10

"That's enough," cried the voice from behind the cellar door.

"Clap, everybody, and shout hooray!"

Clap. Clap. Clap!

"Hooray. Hooray. Hooray!"

"Now comes the best part of the show," the voice continued. "Me, Alinda, the lovely lady singer, who will sing for your pleasure 'On the Sunny Side of the Street.' Everybody say Oh and Ah!"

"Oh!"

"Ah!"

"Oh, ah!"

The cellar door opened and out came
Alinda. She wore a hat with feathers stick-
ing out, a lady's dress, and high-heeled
shoes.

"Hello, everybody!" someone said.

Everybody turned and saw Lenny wearing a fireman's hat.

"Can I play too?" he asked.

"We're not playing," Alinda shouted. "It's a real show and you can't."

"Why?"

"Because."

"Anyway," said Lenny, "I have to go put out a fire. Everybody want to come?"

They all shook their heads no.

14

Lenny ran out of the yard.

"Now I'll sing," Alinda said.

She closed her eyes. "On the sun—"

"Want to know something?" asked Lenny.

He was back again.

"What?" asked Alinda.

"I know a trick," said Lenny.

"What trick?"

15

"First," Lenny explained, "I throw my fireman's hat up in the air and then the one who catches it can keep it. Everybody want to play?"

They all shook their heads yes.

"All right," said Alinda.

Lenny threw the hat high into the air and it landed on Rosie's window ledge.

"How will we catch it now?" Kathy asked.

"We'll have to climb up for it," said Alinda.

So they did. Sal climbed on top of Pudgy. Dolly climbed on top of Sal. Kathy on top of Dolly. Lenny on top of Kathy, and Alinda on top of everybody. She took the fireman's hat off the window ledge and put it on her head.

"I caught it, it's mine," she shouted. "Hooray for me!"

They all climbed down.

"Now I'll sing," Alinda said.

She stretched out her arms. "On the sun—"

"Give me back my hat," said Lenny. "I have to go put out another fire."

"No," said Alinda. "You said for keeps."

"It was only a game," said Lenny, "and my mother says I shouldn't give anything away any more."

He pulled the hat off Alinda's head and ran out of the yard.

"Come on, Pudgy," he called. "Come on, Sal, help me put the fire out!"

"We better help him," said Pudgy.

"He needs us," said Sal.

"But—" Alinda began.

But they were already gone.

"I better go too," said Dolly.

"I didn't sing my song yet," said Alinda.

"I'm hungry," Dolly answered. And she went home.

They were all gone. Two of the folding chairs lay on their sides.

"It's getting late," said Kathy. "I have to go home."

"Wasn't it a wonderful show?" asked Rosie.

"It was the best I ever saw," Kathy answered. "Let's have another one soon."

"Same time, same place," said Rosie.

"Good-by, Cha-Charoo."

"Good-by, Alinda."

Rosie was all alone. She climbed on top of a folding chair and said very quietly, "Ladies and gentlemen, Alinda will now sing 'On the Sunny Side of the Street.'"

And she sang the song all the way to the end.

CHAPTER TWO

There was nothing to do.

"I have nothing to do, Mama," Rosie said.

"Well, do something," her mother said.

So Rosie did something. She wrote a note and pasted it on her front door.

"What did you do?" her mother asked.

"Oh," said Rosie, "I pasted a note on the front door."

"That's nice," her mother said. "Now find something else to do."

Rosie found a red blanket. She put it over her head and sat down on the cellar door in her back yard.

CHAPTER THREE

"Mama," said Kathy, "I have nothing to do."

"Go and play with Dolly," her mother said.

So Kathy went to Dolly's house.

"Hello, Dolly, what are you doing?" she asked.

"I don't know," Dolly answered.

They went to Pudgy's house. He was sitting on the front steps with Sal.

24

"What are you doing?" asked Kathy.

"We're not talking to each other," answered Pudgy.

"That's not doing much," Dolly said.

"What are you doing?" asked Sal.

"Nothing," said Kathy. "We thought you would be doing something."

"What do you want to do?" asked Pudgy.

They all looked at each other. Nobody had anything to say.

"Let's ask Rosie what to do."

So they went to Rosie's house.

"Rosie!" they called.

There was no answer.

"Look," said Kathy, pointing to the note pasted on Rosie's front door.

It said, "If you are looking for me it won't be easy because I am wearing a disguise. Yours truly, Alinda."

"Let's look in the back yard," said Dolly.

They all ran into Rosie's back yard and there, sitting on the cellar door, covered from head to foot in a red blanket, was somebody.

"Is that you, Rosie?" Dolly asked.

26

There was no answer.

"Please tell us who you are," said Kathy.

"I'm Alinda the lost girl."

"Who lost you?" asked Pudgy.

"I lost myself," answered Alinda.

"Aren't you really Rosie though?" asked Pudgy.

"I used to be Rosie," Alinda said, "but not any more."

They all sat down on the cellar door.

"Who is going to find you?" asked Sal.

"Magic Man," said Alinda.

"Who's he?"

"My best friend," answered Alinda.

"And what happens when he finds you?" Kathy asked.

"He will tell me what to do," explained Alinda.

"Can we wait with you?" asked Pudgy.

"I suppose so," said Alinda. "But you must be very quiet."

So they were very quiet. They didn't say a word. They didn't do anything. They just waited.

"This is fun," whispered Kathy.

"SHH-HH!" they all said.

And they were quiet for a long time. Soon it was very late.

"It's very late," Dolly whispered. "I have to go home."

"Me too," said Pudgy.

"I guess Magic Man isn't coming today," said Kathy.

"I guess not," said Alinda.

"Maybe he will come tomorrow," said Sal.

"Maybe," said Alinda. "Maybe not."

"Can we come and wait with you again tomorrow?" Dolly asked.

"I suppose so," said Alinda.

"We'll come earlier tomorrow," said Kathy. "Then we can wait longer."

"Let's all meet at twelve o'clock on Rosie's cellar door," said Pudgy.

"Twelve o'clock sharp!" said Sal.

"Sharp!" they all agreed.

And then they went home.

That evening, when their mothers asked them what they had done all afternoon, they said they had done so much there wasn't even enough time to do it in and they were going to do it all over again tomorrow.

"Good!" all their mothers said.

30

CHAPTER FOUR

"Mama," Rosie asked, "am I your little girl?"

"Of course," her mother answered.

"I mean—" began Rosie.

"You mean this," said her mother, and she gave Rosie three kisses.

"I mean," said Rosie, "can I have a firecracker?"

"No," her mother answered.

"But it's the Fourth of July," said Rosie.

"I know," said her mother.

"Kathy and Dolly have firecrackers," said Rosie.

"I don't believe that," her mother answered. "They are dangerous and I do not want my little girl to get hurt."

"I am not your little girl," said Rosie. "I'm a big girl and everybody else has firecrackers."

"I don't believe that," her mother said.

Rosie didn't say a word.

"Play with your cat Buttermilk," said her mother. "That would be much nicer."

"I don't believe that," said Rosie.

"What did you say?" her mother asked.

Rosie went out and sat on the steps in front of her house.

It was twelve o'clock. Kathy, Dolly, Pudgy, and Sal came and stood in front of her.

"It's twelve o'clock," said Kathy. "Time to wait for Magic Man."

Rosie went back into the house and put on her red blanket. When she came out, everybody was already seated on the cellar door in the back yard. She sat down next to them. Nobody said a word.

"Will he soon be here, Rosie?" Dolly asked.

"My name is Alinda," said Rosie.

"—Alinda?"

"I don't know," said Alinda.

"We'd better be quiet," Pudgy whispered.

They were quiet. Rosie's cat Buttermilk meowed softly and crept into her lap. The moments went by.

"I hear someone coming. Quick," said
Alinda, "shut your eyes everybody!"

They shut their eyes.

"Hello, it's me. What's the matter with
everybody?"

Everybody opened his eyes. It was Lenny
wearing a cowboy hat.

"If you want to wait with us," said Alinda,
"sit down and be quiet."

"All right," said Lenny. He sat down.

"What are we waiting for?" he asked.

"Magic Man," Pudgy whispered.

"Oh," said Lenny. "Who's—?"

"SHH-HH!"

They were quiet again.

"I think I saw the leaves move just a little bit," whispered Dolly.

"He's really coming now," said Alinda. "Shut your eyes again!"

They all shut their eyes again. They all held hands. They listened.

They heard Alinda say, "Hello, Magic Man—Oh, how nice—thank you so much.

"Good-by, and please give my regards to your wife."

They were quiet for a little. Then, "Can we open our eyes now?" Kathy asked.

"Yes," said Alinda.

"I didn't see him," said Lenny.

"Your eyes were shut," said Dolly.

"He was very quiet," said Sal.

"Did he wear a cowboy hat?" Lenny asked.

"Yes," said Alinda.

Everybody shouted at the same time.

"And a mask?"

"And wings?"

"And a blue cape?"

"And earmuffs?"

"Of course," said Alinda.

"Then it really was Magic Man!" Lenny shouted.

"Of course," they all agreed.

"What did he tell you, Alinda?" asked Kathy.

"He told me that I'm not Alinda the lost girl any more."

"What else?" asked Pudgy.

"And he told me—"

"What?" they all shouted.

"He told me that I could be a big red firecracker!"

"Ohh!"

"And he told me—"

"What?" they all shouted.

"He told me that all of you could be little silver firecrackers!"

"Boom!" shouted Dolly.

"Crack-phizz-boom!" shouted Kathy.

"Whizz-bam-boom!" shouted Pudgy and Sal.

"And he told me—"

"What?" they all shouted.

"He told me that we could be firecrackers for the whole Fourth of July day!"

"Hooray for Magic Man!"

Lenny jumped high in the air.

"Here I come," he said. "Whizzzz-boom!"

Sal stood on his head and said, "I didn't go off yet."

Kathy and Dolly danced in a circle singing, "Boom-te-de-boom-boom."

Rosie climbed to the top of the cellar door and yelled, "I'm the biggest
red firecracker in the whole world and
here I go! BOOMM! BOOMM-BOOMM-
aWHISHHHH!"

They jumped, they ran, they skipped out
of Rosie's back yard.

They phizzed, they whizzed, they crack-
led all the way home.

43

Buttermilk meowed softly.

"Are you tired, honey?" Rosie asked. "Come on, let's go in the house."

She picked up the cat and knocked on the door. KNOCK-KNOCK.

"Who's there?" asked her mother.

"It's Alinda, the lovely lady singer," said Rosie.

"I don't believe that," her mother answered.

44

"It's Alinda the lost girl," said Rosie.

"I don't believe that either," her mother said.

"It's Alinda the big red firecracker and I'm going to blow the whole house down."

"Don't do that," said her mother, and she opened the door.

"Rosie!" she said.

"Didn't you know it was me?" asked Rosie.

45

"I thought so," her mother said, "but I wasn't sure."

"I'm tired, Mama," said Rosie. "Buttermilk is tired too. We had a big Fourth of July day."

"I can believe that," her mother said. "Why don't you both go to sleep?"

Rosie picked up the cat and went upstairs to her room. In a little while her mother went up to see if they were asleep. She opened the door and saw Buttermilk in bed with the blanket pulled up to his chin and Rosie curled up on the rug.

"Rosie!" she said.

"Shh!" said Rosie. "Buttermilk is asleep."

"Why are you on the floor, dear?" her mother whispered.

"Because I'm a sleepy cat," answered Rosie.

46

"Oh," said her mother, and she tiptoed out of the room.

"Good night," she whispered as she closed the door.

"Meow," answered Rosie.